To Brandon and Ethan

Special thanks to Brandon Rodshaw

Bloomsbury Publishing, London, Berlin, New York and Sydney

First published in Great Britain in February 2012 by Bloomsbury Publishing Plc
50 Bedford Square, London, WC1B 3DP

A CIP catalogue record for this book is available from the British Library

ISBN 978 1 4088 1580 9

Typeset by Hewer Text UK Ltd, Edinburgh
Printed in Great Britain by Clays Ltd, St Ives Plc, Bungay, Suffolk

1 3 5 7 9 10 8 6 4 2

www.bloomsbury.com
www.starfighterbooks.com

MAX CHASE

BLOOMSBURY

LONDON BERLIN NEW YORK SYDNEY

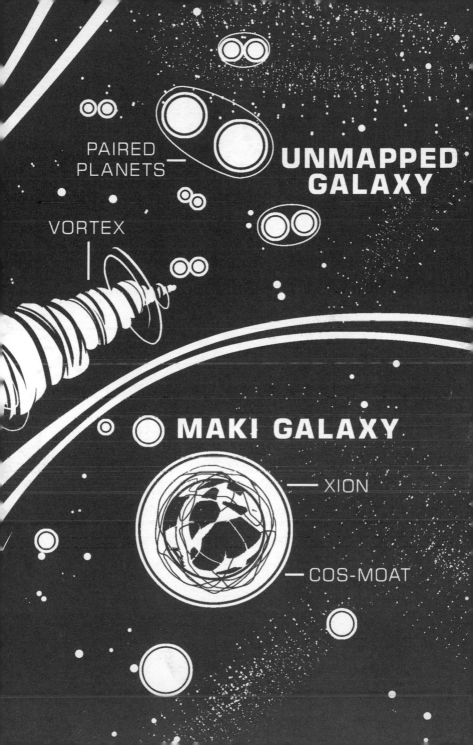

STAR FIGHTERS

An elite fighting team sworn to protect and defend the galaxy

It is the year 5012 and the Milky Way galaxy is under attack . . .

After the Universal War . . . a war that almost brought about the destruction of every known universe . . . the planets in the Milky Way banded together to create the Intergalactic Force – an elite fighting team sworn to protect and defend the galaxy.

Only the brightest and most promising students are accepted into the Intergalactic Force Academy, and only the very best cadets reach the highest of their ranks and become . . .

To be a Star Fighter is to dedicate your life to one mission: *Peace in Space*. They are given the coolest weapons, the fastest spaceships – and the most dangerous missions. Everyone at the Intergalactic Force Academy wants to be a Star Fighter someday.

Do YOU have what it takes?

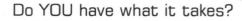

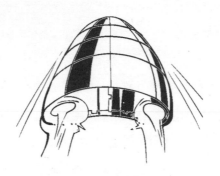

Chapter 1

'That treacherous double-crossing snake in the grass!' Diesel slammed his fist into the wall as he and Peri walked along the corridor that led to the Bridge of the *Phoenix*.

'I don't think they have grass on Meigwor,' Peri said.

'What do they have?' asked Diesel.

Peri shrugged. 'Trees, mostly. It's a jungle planet.'

'Snake in the trees, then. Let's push Otto into the air-lock and out into space and let the space-sharks chew on his big, long, rubbery neck!'

The strip of hair on Diesel's head was bristling like a Betelgeusian Pinfish's spines, and glowing bright orange, as it always did when the half-Martian was really angry.

They had just survived a dangerous mission on the planet Xion, supposedly to rescue a kidnapped Meigwor prince. The Meigwor had sent Otto, a bounty hunter, to lead the mission, but he had lied to Diesel and Peri. They had raided the Xion palace and captured someone, but it wasn't a *Meigwor* prince.

They hadn't rescued anyone – they had in fact *kidnapped* a Xion prince!

'Let's give him what he deserves –' Diesel said.

Peri held up his hand. 'If we throw Otto

to the space-sharks, the Meigwor will take it out on Selene.' Their friend was being held on Otto's home planet. 'It's time we stopped letting Otto boss us around. We need to rescue Selene and then return Prince Onix to Xion.'

'Otto won't back down without a fight.'

'Then we'll give him a fight!' Peri said. 'There are two of us – we should be able to disarm Otto and take back our ship.'

They were nearly at the Bridge now. Peri touched a button on the belt of his Expedition Wear. Diesel did the same. The surfaces of their suits became hard and shiny, like armour. Steel gauntlets emerged from the sleeves and covered their hands. Plexiglas helmets rose from the necks of the suits, encasing their heads in identical transparent, armoured bubbles.

'We might need more protection,' Peri said.

He touched the wall and a section slid smoothly back to reveal a chamber filled with vaporisers, blasters, phasers and jellifiers in countless different shapes and sizes.

'Look,' Peri said. 'Otto's been here.' He pointed to a silver flask on a shelf. It was the flask in which Otto kept his favourite drink, Meigwor Mudcreeper's Blood. Peri grimaced. 'Dunno how he can drink that stuff.'

Diesel picked up a little black weapon, with a wide, square muzzle. 'I've seen these in the training manual,' Diesel said. 'It's a duster.'

Diesel took aim at Otto's flask. He pressed the trigger. The flask dissolved into a small heap of fine grey dust.

'Wow,' Peri said. 'Better not use that unless it's life or death.' He picked up a handful of green pellets, about the size of acorns. 'I recognise these – Paralysides, aren't they?'

Diesel nodded. 'Chuck one at someone and it'll leave them totally immobilised for up to an hour.'

'That's more like it,' Peri said. 'We could use these on Otto, if we have to.'

They filled their pockets with the pellets. They both took a duster, too, just for show.

'Come on,' Peri said. 'It's sorting-Otto-out-time!'

When they reached the door to the Bridge, Peri heard shouting. He caught Diesel's arm. 'It sounds like more than one voice.'

'Maybe Otto's listening to the Sonicwave System,' Diesel said. 'Perhaps that's what Meigwor music sounds like.'

The doors to the Bridge slid open. Peri saw three huge Xion guards attacking Otto. They were dressed in black battle gear that made them look like giant insects. Each carried an electric mace in his clawed hands. They swiped viciously at Otto, who was dodging desperately, his crimson neck swaying from side to side. He fired a constant stream of laser blasts at the intruders. Every time a Xion guard was hit he staggered back and screamed, before returning to the attack. Otto was holding them off, but he wouldn't be able to keep it up for much longer.

Peri and Diesel looked at each other.

'How did they find us?' Diesel asked.

Peri shrugged. 'We've got their prince. We should have expected they'd track us to the ends of the universe.'

'What do we do?' Diesel asked.

Peri's instinct was to fight the invaders. On the other hand, Otto did deserve a little punishment for kidnapping their prince.

'Leave them to it,' Peri said. 'How did they get on board, anyway?'

As if in answer, a patch of air ahead of them began fizzing. The air crackled and started to swirl, then turned black

and solidified into another Xion guard, swinging an electric mace.

Peri felt as if his guts had turned to iced water. There was no one at the controls. Otto was too busy trying to fight off the intruders. With nobody at the helm, the ship could hit an asteroid or a planet, or drift too close to a star and be sucked in by its gravity.

Another three Xion guards teleported aboard and dived into Otto's scrum.

'We have to go in,' Peri said.

Diesel cracked his knuckles and curled his hands into fists.

Another four Xion guards teleported aboard, and this time they turned towards Peri and Diesel.

Chapter 2

Peri grabbed a handful of the Paralyside pellets and threw them at the feet of the nearest Xion guards. The pellets exploded with sharp *cracks*. Tiny flames sprang up where they landed. Coils of grey smoke swirled around the targets.

'Switch on your Atmos-Filter!' Peri shouted to Diesel. He touched the side of his Expedition Wear helmet. Nose-plugs were immediately inserted into his nostrils.

The two guards nearest Peri slumped to the floor. Peri lunged for the control panel,

which slid the extra distance to meet him, as if reading his thoughts. Peri was half-bionic and programmed to work with the *Phoenix*. His fingers danced across the console as he set the ship to automatic pilot, bound for Meigwor.

Diesel hurled more Paralysides at the guards. They collapsed like Procyonian Nightbirds at dawn.

A pellet landed near Otto, who wasn't wearing Expedition Wear. 'Hey!' he shouted. 'Don't chuck them at me, you –'

He swayed and crashed to the floor in a heap with all the Xion guards. Diesel stepped between the intruders' limp claws and high-fived Peri.

'That sorted them out!'

'Yup!' Peri said. He nudged the motion-less guards with the toe of his Expedition Wear boot. 'I know you can hear me. This is what happens when you come barging on to someone else's ship without being invited. Now, about your prince. There was a bit of a misunderstanding, and —'

'No misunderstanding,' growled one of the Xions. 'You take our prince, you die.'

'They shouldn't be able to talk, should they?' Peri whispered to Diesel.

Diesel was examining the spent casing of one of the Paralyside pellets. 'They're only Level One Paralysides,' he said. 'Low strength. The effect only lasts a few seconds.'

'Oh, that's great,' Peri muttered.

The guard who had spoken was already hauling himself to his feet. 'Prepare for the ultimate punishment. For Xion!'

All the other guards were slowly getting up. 'For Xion!' they echoed.

Peri reached in his pocket for more Paralyside pellets.

He had only one left.

Diesel drew the duster from his belt.

'Isn't that a bit harsh?' Peri asked Diesel.

The Xion guard who'd been the first to recover swung his electric mace at Peri's head. Peri ducked. He heard the crackle and felt the heat as it passed just over his scalp.

Peri backed away and aimed his duster at the guard. 'Look, I don't want to shoot, but –'

The guard came towards him, jabbing with the mace.

Peri couldn't bring himself to press the trigger. The Xion were only trying to rescue their kidnapped prince. Peri took the duster by the end and swung it at the guard.

The guard threw his arm up to protect his face. The duster smashed into his wrist, where he wore a band with a bright orange button. The Xion's eyes widened. He grew blurry at the edges, fizzled, then winked out of existence.

Peri realised he must have hit the guard's teleportation device.

'Diesel!' he shouted. 'Hit their teleport buttons! On the wrist!'

All the remaining guards were on their feet now. They still looked groggy, but they meant business. Some advanced on Peri and Diesel while others pounced on Otto's lifeless body.

Diesel struck at the nearest guard's wrist. The guard fizzled and then vanished.

Another guard thrust his mace at Peri, who dodged out of the way. The crackling mace flashed past his helmet. While the guard was still off balance, Peri knocked his wristband with the butt of the duster. The guard disappeared.

That was three less to deal with. But it was still Peri and Diesel against eight Xion guards. Peri wished Otto would snap out of it and help them. Their only chance was to hit the guards before they'd fully recovered.

Peri's arms tingled and his legs throbbed. He felt his muscles expanding inside his suit. His bionic abilities were kicking in. Moving at super-speed, he slid under the flailing mace of one guard and hit the teleportation device. Then he did the same to another, and another, in quick succession. Diesel, meanwhile, had managed to teleport one. There were now only four guards left.

'Nice work, Diesel!' Peri shouted. 'Let's just mop these last ones up.'

He ducked under the sweep of another guard's mace and teleported him too. But at the same moment, the biggest and fiercest-looking Xion guard gave Otto one swift kick and then leapt up. He jabbed his electric mace at Peri, piercing his Expedition Wear.

Peri's stomach felt as if it had been scorched with a flame-thrower. He shouted a wordless cry. The duster fell from his nerveless hand. He dropped to his knees.

'Peri!' Diesel called and levelled his duster at the Xion who had injured his friend.

Peri saw the towering guard ram his electric mace into Diesel's duster and thrust forward, catching him on the arm. Diesel collapsed.

'So fall all enemies of the mighty Xion!' boomed the guard.

The electric mace had done something serious to Peri. He could feel it – not just the pain but a surge through his veins and wires in equal measure. *The electric shock's messed up my circuitry,* he thought. There was a downside to being half-bionic and half-boy. Not only could you feel pain, but you could get short-circuited too.

'Where is Prince Onix?' shouted the biggest, fiercest guard. He wore a purple star on his chest, which indicated he was the general.

Peri could hardly turn his head but he slowly scanned the Bridge. Diesel was huddled on the floor next to him, but Otto was nowhere to be seen.

Typical Otto! He was only out for himself. Peri and Diesel had saved him from the guards and in return he'd left them in the lurch. Peri wished Otto had been the one to get hit with an electric mace.

'You dare to defy me, General Dachkor, Xion warrior.' He picked up Peri's duster. 'What is this? A duster? These are good. Oh, yes, you can do a lot with a duster.' He pointed it at Peri. 'If I press the trigger now, your head will crumble to dust. Tell me where the prince is and you shall live.'

But the anger in the general's face, the way his finger twitched on the trigger, told a different story. As soon as the general knew where the prince was, he'd kill them. Peri was sure of it.

Another guard picked up the other fallen duster and pointed it at Diesel.

Peri saw that the strip of hair on top of Diesel's head had turned a dull grey and was lying flat.

Peri managed to mutter to Otto: 'Donut tell.' His mouth wasn't working properly. His tongue felt thick and clumsy.

'I've got a good idea,' said the general. He pushed the duster closer to Peri's face. 'I will get rid of you, and then your friend can tell us.'

Peri opened his mouth. If he could just explain that the kidnapping wasn't their idea, it was Otto's . . . But the words wouldn't come. And the general would never have believed him anyway.

Peri closed his eyes and prepared to turn to dust.

Chapter 3

'Hold it right there!' said a loud, booming voice.

Peri opened his eyes again.

He had never imagined being pleased to see Otto. The Meigwor bounty hunter stood in the doorway, one long crimson arm coiled round Prince Onix.

'Release those Earthlings at once!' Otto shouted.

Diesel scoffed. 'Excuse me, I'm half-Martian!'

The Xion general aimed his duster gun

at Otto. 'I don't think so. Let go of the prince or be pulverised!'

Otto pushed the prince in front of him. 'Yeah, that's a good idea. Press the trigger and pulverise your prince!'

General Dachkor lowered his gun uncertainly, looking round at his fellow guards for help. They looked as confused as he did.

'Slide your weapons over the floor towards me!' Otto yelled.

There was a long, tense pause.

Otto tightened his grip around the prince.

'Do as he says!' the prince screamed.

The general shoved the duster over the floor towards Otto. The other weapons quickly followed, clattering at Otto's feet.

Peri stood up and moved away from the general. He still didn't feel quite connected to his limbs — there was a delay between his brain telling his legs to move and them actually doing it.

'Thanks, Otto,' Diesel said through gritted teeth.

'Whatever!' Otto mumbled. He picked up a duster and trained it on General Dachkor's face. 'Now who's going to be pulverised?!'

'Mo! Datta be sloopid fling to do!' Peri's mouth still wasn't working.

'What did you say?!' Otto asked, puzzled.

Peri growled in frustration. He had to stop Otto – if Otto killed the guards, he would start an all-out intergalactic war.

If words weren't working, maybe actions would.

Peri launched himself across the room. He crashed into Otto. The duster flew from Otto's hand. Diesel swiftly scooped it up.

'You stupid inferior life form!' Otto shouted. His eyes bulged with fury. He let go of the prince and shoved Peri into the control panel.

The control panel cracked Peri in the back and he felt a power surge inside him, as if something had been switched on. 'Ow! What did you do that for, you – Hey! I can speak properly!'

Diesel darted to the nearest guard and slapped his teleportation device. He fizzled and disappeared. The others backed away. Diesel pointed the duster gun at them. They froze.

Peri pressed the teleportation buttons of two of the remaining guards. They, too, disappeared. The Bridge was starting to feel empty.

Only General Dachkor remained. He lunged forward and grabbed the prince, holding him tightly with one arm. 'Victory to Xion!' he shouted as he pressed the orange button on his wrist.

Otto's long arm snaked out and snatched the general's teleportation band right off his wrist. But it was too late. The general began to fizzle at the edges. Otto grabbed Prince Onix's ankles.

General Dachkor winked out of existence. So did the top half of the prince's body.

But his legs were still on the Bridge, gripped by Otto.

'*Ch'ach!*' said Diesel. 'The prince has been torn in two!'

'No he hasn't,' Peri said, stepping towards Otto and the pair of legs that were kicking and wriggling. He could see a thin ring of bright white light where the prince's upper body would begin – if it was still there.

Peri grabbed on to the prince's legs.

'Diesel,' he said. 'Help me pull the prince back!'

'Why?' asked the half-Martian. 'Shouldn't we just let the Xion take him? They won't attack us then!'

'But we can't save Selene without him!' Peri said.

'Good point,' Diesel said, reaching forward to help tug at the prince's flailing legs.

'Almost got him!' Otto cried as, with an ear-rattling *whoosh*, the prince came sliding through the ring of white light, back on to the Bridge.

'Are you OK?' Peri asked him. 'Do your legs work?'

The prince stumbled around, his legs somehow both stiff and wobbly. 'Yes. But that won't save you!' His eyes flashed bright amber. 'You've kidnapped a prince of the blood royal, you've tied me up, you've torn me in two —'

'But we put you back together again,' Peri reminded him, as he tapped a button on the side of his Expedition Wear. The helmet retracted and his Expedition Wear armour softened. He heard Diesel doing the same.

'You think my people will let this insult go unavenged? They will go to the ends of the universe to find you. They will throw you into the Sludge Mines —'

'Hey!' Diesel said. 'Don't blame us. If your people want to send someone to the Sludge Mines, send *him*.' He pointed at Otto. Otto glared back.

'It's true,' Peri said. 'We didn't know what he was up to.' He took a step towards the bounty hunter. 'But he's not in charge any more.' Peri grabbed the Xion teleportation band from the Meigwor. 'I'll take that.' He placed his hand on the wall of the Bridge. 'Bits and bobs,' Peri said to the *Phoenix*. A drawer popped out. It held all kinds of useful things, and could be accessed from any part of the ship. Peri dropped the teleportation band into it for safe keeping. 'Lock drawer.'

Peri started to realise just what a mess Otto had got them into. 'We're not going along with your evil plans any more, Otto.

We're going to Meigwor and we're getting Selene back. Then we're taking the prince back to Xion. No more of your stupid tricks!'

Otto stood as still as a stone, his mouth hanging open. Peri thought maybe he was finally getting through to him.

But Diesel's mouth was hanging open, too. His strip of hair had turned white. They were both staring at something behind Peri.

Peri turned round.

There, in the middle of the 360-monitor, hung the sinister shape of a Xion battle-ship. Just like the one that obliterated the IF Space Station. It was very, very, very, very, very big.

And getting closer by the second.

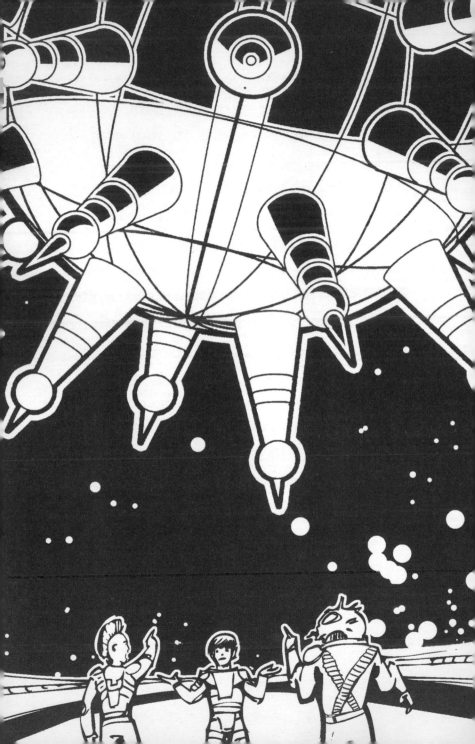

Chapter 4

'You see?' said Prince Onix triumphantly. 'You really thought you could get away with kidnapping me, without my people coming after you?'

'They won't dare blow us up with you on board,' Diesel said.

'No, they won't,' the prince agreed. 'They'll capture the ship and take you back to Xion, and then it's the Sludge Mines for you.'

Peri looked again at the battleship hanging in the blackness of space. A grid of glowing white rays projected from it. He knew what it was — he had read about it in training at the Intergalactic Force Academy. A Laser Cage. In a few seconds, it would close around them.

'Do something!' Otto yelled.

Peri dived for the control panel. He had to engage the ship's Superluminal speed, and fast. It didn't matter where they went as long as it was a long, long way away from here.

His hands hovered above the controls — and stopped. He couldn't remember what to do. What had the electric mace done to him? Something was definitely wrong with his connection to the *Phoenix*.

'Hurry up!' Diesel shouted.

The glowing lines of the Laser Cage now filled the 360-monitor.

Peri forced himself to think, which he'd

never had to do before when it came to the *Phoenix*. His parents had designed him to operate the ship and it had always come as second nature to him. He didn't have to think what to do; he just did it. Now he concentrated and remembered that the touchpad for Superluminal speed was the glowing red one. He placed his palm on the red screen. The panel clicked and then glided open. Inside were two switches. His trembling fingers flicked them just in time.

The Xion battleship became a dot on the 360-monitor. Then nothing.

Planets and suns flashed past. Space was mostly empty, and there were light years of nothingness between solar systems. But at Superluminal speed, light years were covered in seconds.

Peri tugged at the Nav-wheel, frantically swerving and dipping. It was much harder

now his connection to the *Phoenix* was
scrambled. Sweat formed on his brow and
dripped down his temple. Giant spheres of
rock and even gianter balls of blazing
hydrogen rushed towards them.

He remembered he must check the Velocity
View. A huge yellow star rapidly filled the
screen. They were heading straight for it.
They'd be burned to a crisp. Or to a vapour.

Peri screwed his eyes shut against the

searing glare. The 360-monitor tinted. He disengaged Superluminal speed. He wrenched the Nav-wheel. Diesel was screaming. Then . . .

Nothing.

Peri opened his eyes. The star was a nice, safe distance away, still glowing. 'Whew!' he said shakily.

The *Phoenix* was orbiting around a planet with orange land masses, purple oceans and wisps of green cloud.

'I thought we were goners,' Diesel said.

Peri glanced around the Bridge and realised what was missing. 'Where are Otto and the prince?'

Diesel looked high and low. There was no sign of the Meigwor or the Xion.

'What's Otto up to now?' Diesel groaned.

'He must have some sneaky plan,' Peri said. 'He always does.'

'Should we go after him?'

Peri shook his head. 'We don't want to start playing hide-and-seek. Now we've got a bit of time to ourselves, let's work out a plan to rescue Selene.'

Diesel's strip of hair faded from red to pink to purple 'Can't you use the *Phoenix* to send Selene a message? I mean, it must have lots of data about Selene stored.'

'Good idea,' Peri paused. 'But how?'

'You're the one who's supposed to understand this ship.'

Peri nodded. Normally he understood the ship completely. But right now his mind was blank.

'I don't know,' he said. 'I can't think.'

Diesel's strip of hair flared bright pink again. 'Selene's wearing her Expedition Wear, right?'

'Right.'

'Can't the ship use that to locate her?'

'That's not a bad idea,' Peri said. Why hadn't he thought of it? If Diesel could out-think him, his circuits must have been badly scrambled by that shock from the electric mace. Otto had repaired some of the damage when he'd shoved him against the console, but he still wasn't right. He was beginning to wonder if his bionic half would ever work properly again.

'The suits are coded, right?' Diesel continued. 'Each one has a number.' Diesel pulled at a label stitched to his forearm. 'Mine's #4737.3.'

'#4737.6,' Peri said, looking at his own label.

'So Selene's must be either #4737.0, or #4737.9.'

'Right.' Peri tried to think how the ship's

computer could use that information. But it was like trying to peer through fog. He knew the answer was there, but he just couldn't see it.

Diesel rolled his eyes. 'What's the matter with you? We use the Quikmap function, dumboid!'

'Oh, yeah,' Peri said. 'I was just going to say that.'

They stood together at the control panel – a huge bank of buttons and dials and touchpads and keypads and winking lights and screens and displays.

'So where's the Quikmap function?' Diesel asked.

'Er –' Peri fingered a switch and then a dial. He couldn't remember which button to use. He couldn't imagine what hitting the wrong button might do. He knew they hadn't discovered one millionth of what the *Phoenix* could do. One button might tuck them into their sleeping pods while another might be the self-destruct sequence. He didn't know. He hadn't realised how much being half-bionic had helped him know instinctively how the *Phoenix* worked. It had felt so natural, and now he felt empty somehow.

'This must be it!' Diesel pointed at a screen that had an icon of a solar system above it. 'Set it for planetary level, right?'

'Yeah,' Peri said, but he wasn't sure, not really.

'And home in on Meigwor?'

'That's where she is, so . . .'

Diesel flicked through the images on the touchpad until Meigwor, a greenish ball with muddy brown oceans floating in the blackness of space, appeared on the screen.

'Closer Search Function,' Diesel read

from a message that had appeared at the top of the screen. 'Do you think that's it?'

'Must be.'

Diesel touched the message. A keypad appeared in its place. 'I'll try the suit numbers.'

'I can do that.' Peri nudged Diesel aside and typed in the suit number. He missed the hum he used to feel when he touched the control panel.

The image of Meigwor rapidly filled the screen. The image came into focus as the Quikmap orb reached the surface of the planet. It whizzed round and round Meigwor at a million miles an hour, transmitting pictures to the Quikmap screen. They flickered past so fast Peri could barely make them out. He just caught the odd detail here and there – a bubbling brown ocean, then, a nanosecond later, a city with strange, squat buildings. Then pictures of steamy jungle flickered past. The trees had round purple-and-green leaves. There were fluttering insects as big as birds. Peri caught a glimpse of a weird, red creature without a head.

Then, in a clearing, a figure clothed in Expedition Wear.

'There she is!' Peri shouted.

No doubt about it. Peri saw her face clearly. Her cheeks were flushed, her hair clung damply to the side of her face. She was looking around nervously, biting her lip.

From out of the surrounding jungle, Meigwor soldiers advanced.

Ten of them. Some held laserpulses. Some held curved, scythe-like swords. Their long, red necks craned towards Selene.

They closed in on her. Selene looked

wildly around. But there was nowhere for her to run.

The monitor fogged up and then flickered off.

'She's in trouble,' Peri said. 'We have to get there now!'

Chapter 5

'I'll plot a course for Selene's location,' Peri said, trying to sound more confident than he felt.

'I'll go look for Otto and the prince,' Diesel said, hurrying towards the nearest portal. It opened with a hiss. Diesel clumped down the corridor.

Peri searched the console for the Pinpoint Navigational Keypad. There it was: a milky-white window with a keypad of letters, numbers and symbols. To plot a course for the right section of the Meigwor

jungle he'd have to input the space coordinates for where they'd just seen Selene.
How would he find those?

There had to be a quicker way of doing
this. If he was his normal self, he'd know it
intuitively.

The shipboard monitor on the far wall
glowed into life. Peri saw Diesel standing
by a glittering blue swimming pool. 'Hey,
Peri, check this out!' Diesel said and flipped
some sort of Remote Transfigurator
Device. At once the pool closed over and a
full-sized Neptunian quarkball court
sprang into view.

'Cool, isn't it? You can go for a swim or
play quarkball. This ship's got all kinds of
stuff!'

'I'm so glad you're having a nice time,'
Peri said. 'But shouldn't you be looking for
Otto and Onix?'

'Yeah, yeah, I'll find them, don't worry.'

Peri returned his attention to the console. There was a glowing purple button marked *Oracle*. He touched it.

A shimmering panel of rainbow light appeared in the air in front of him. 'Please pose your question,' it said in a soothing deep voice.

'Space coordinates for most recent location of Expedition Wear 4737.0, please.'

'Easy-peasy,' the Oracle said. '10101010 11100110001zxfxfzbluedogpqr and fifty-seven and a half.'

'Er, thanks,' Peri said. 'Sorry, do you think you could repeat that?'

The shipboard monitor panel glowed into life again.

'Hey, look at this!' Diesel said. He was standing in a dark auditorium with antique-style anchored seats and a big screen at the front. On the screen were moving pictures of a cowboy and a quaint, old-fashioned cartoon spaceman figure. 'We've got an old-time cinema on board, how about that? 3-D, computer-generated graphics. Can you believe how primitive entertainment on Earth used to be?'

'Great,' Peri said with a roll of his eyes. 'Shall I come down and watch it with you?'

'Aren't you busy?'

'Yes, I am!' Peri shouted. Martians just didn't get sarcasm. 'And so are you! Find Otto!'

'All right, all right,' Diesel said. 'Keep your wig on.'

Peri returned his attention to the Oracle. 'Could I have those coordinates again? A bit slower?'

The Oracle repeated the coordinates. Peri only just managed to key them in. *Hope*

I haven't got them wrong, he thought, as he engaged the ship's Thruster Control and saw the ship speed forward.

A portal opened and Diesel appeared with Otto and Prince Onix. They were both gagged and bound with lengths of adhesive silicon hemp. All three were shivering. Prince Onix's teeth chattered, and Diesel's strip of hair had turned a pale, arctic blue. Otto glared at his captor.

'Nice one,' Peri said. 'How d'you catch them?'

'Easy for someone with my super-advanced combat skills,' Diesel said. 'Plus a bit of good old Martian cunning. Not everyone could have carried it off, of course, but I have the qualities to –'

'Brag about it later,' Peri said. 'Just tell me what happened.'

'Oh,' said Diesel. 'I found them in the library.'

'The *Phoenix* has a library? With real, actual, paper books?'

'Thousands of them. It's like some crazy old museum. Anyway, I did something really clever.'

'I bet you did.' Peri shook his head, growing sorry he'd asked.

'I remembered what happened when we lowered the temperature to hide Otto from the Xion Toll-Takers. Meigwors can't take the cold – they go all sluggish, remember? So I turned down the thermo in the library to sub-zero. I snuck in and climbed on top of a bookcase and let him have it with the heaviest book I could find – *The Complete History of Intergalactic Conflict*, all two thousand four hundred and twenty-three pages of it. I thumped him right on the head. Just in case the prince started causing trouble, I hit him with *The Stupendous Compendium of Intelligent Life Forms, Volumes 1 to 13*.'

'And then you tied them up? Where did you get the rope?'

'Used the library's Auto-Silencer. Ties and gags anyone making a noise.'

Peri had no idea the library had an Auto-Silencer. He hadn't even known the *Phoenix* had a library. He should have known – or at least not been surprised to find out. *There's no doubt about it*, he thought. *My connection with the ship is gone.*

'Awesome of me, wasn't it?' Diesel said.

'Yeah, whatever.' Peri shrugged. 'While you were off having an ice-tea party with Otto and Onix, I found the coordinates for where Selene is on Meigwor, and we're headed there right now at . . .' He checked the Velocity View. '. . . a hundred thousand miles a second . . . No, wait a minute, eighty thousand miles a second. No, I mean fifty thousand miles a second . . .'

The numbers on the dial were decreasing as he spoke.

'What's going on?' Diesel asked.

Peri tapped the Velocity View as the numbers clicked down. He had no idea what was happening. Could Otto have sabotaged the ship? But that was impossible. He wasn't smart enough. Plus, he'd had no opportunity.

The Velocity View read 0 miles per second now.

Peri scanned the 360-monitor. The infinite blackness of space surrounded them, and countless stars glowed like tiny floating jewels in the distance.

And right in front of the ship, was something very strange.

'Diesel,' said Peri in a low voice. 'I'm seeing things, aren't I? That's not really a giant red thumb, floating in space . . . is it?'

'*Ch'aƈh!*' Diesel said, running his hand through his now yellow strip of hair. 'That's an intergalactic hitchhiking device. I've heard of them; they force passing ships to stop. It's the first one I've ever seen.'

The thumb curled up and seemed to

flick something invisible in the direction of the *Phoenix*. A moment later there was a *Ping!* and a string of words appeared on the Bridge, hovering in the air like black, unwavering smoke.

MY NAME IS KAHATAMA, FROM THE PLANET FOOSWAYLIA. MY SHIP IS DAMAGED AND MY NUTRITIONAL SUPPLIES ARE RUNNING LOW. GOING ANYWHERE NEAR MEIGWOR?

Peri read and reread the message. The 360-monitor flashed as information from *The Space Spotter's Guide* appeared. *The Space Spotter's Guide* contained info on all the life forms, guns and gadgets they were likely to find in the furthest, darkest corners of space.

Fooswaylia

GALAXY: Granxiore

SPECIES: Fooswaylian.

TRAITS: Peaceful, herbivore

THREAT LEVEL: Minimal

Diesel grabbed the control panel and started to engage thrusters.

'Wait.' Peri brushed Diesel's hands away. 'We have to help him, don't we?'

'Are you crazy? We have enough to cope with already!'

'We can't just leave him out there.' Peri grabbed Diesel's arm and ushered him out of earshot of Otto and the prince. 'That's not the Intergalactic Force way. We help those in trouble. It might be a long time before another ship comes along. Like, a few thousand years.'

He located the Universal Message Transmitter on the console and typed: *Welcome aboard.*

Then he lowered the *Phoenix*'s shields.

The thumb exploded in a shower of red stars, which faded and disappeared.

A moment later, there was another passenger on the Bridge.

Chapter 6

The new arrival was one of the strangest creatures Peri had ever seen. And the most colourful. His skin was sky blue. His hair and beard were green. His eyes — all seven of them — were pink. He was wearing red shorts and a golden vest. He had no legs or arms that Peri could see — just two big feet that poked out of the shorts, and two hands that poked out of the sleeves of the vest. He was short, reaching only to Peri's chest. He looked rather like a multi-coloured penguin.

'Oh, you saved me!' he said. His voice sounded like a swarm of crickets having an argument with a swarm of bees. 'Oh, my lovely saviours, my oh-so-special saviours!'

'It was nothing,' Peri said. 'Anyone would have —'

'Oh no, you are special. So trusting and generous,' the Fooswaylian said, and waddled towards Peri and Diesel at surprising speed.

His flipper-like hands extended and hugged them together tightly. He jumped up and down, making Peri and Diesel bounce up and down with him.

'*S'fâh!*' said Diesel. 'There's no need to —'

The Fooswaylian backed off. He was smiling. Peri shuddered. There was something unpleasant about the little alien's smile. And not just because his teeth were maroon.

Peri heard what sounded like a low chuckle from Otto. It was hard to be sure because of the gag, but Otto appeared to be grinning.

'What's going on?' Peri asked. He tried to move towards Otto, but was immediately pulled back. A strange, sticky purple gel had glued him to Diesel. They were literally joined at the hip.

'What is this stuff?' Diesel shouted in disgust.

'Fooswaylia one, Earth nil!' sang the Fooswaylian.

He waddled over to Otto, ungagging and untying him. Then Otto and the Fooswaylian did a strange, shuffling dance together, which ended with them touching noses.

'Thanks, Kahatama!' Otto's voice echoed around the Bridge. 'Smooth work!' Otto smacked his hands together over his head in salute. He smiled a lipless smile at Peri and Diesel. 'It's good to see you two have become so close!'

'Don't mess about, Otto!' Peri screamed. 'Let us go!'

'You thought you could outsmart me? The greatest bounty hunter in the history of the universe? The most cunning, ruthless, unstoppable –'

'This is getting boring.' Diesel yawned. 'Can't we skip this bit?'

'Don't get cheeky with me!' Otto stopped smiling. His eyes bulged like a pair of Krespossian Water-Figs. 'You two space-monkeys are going to fly me home and we're going to hand over the prince to the Meigwor authorities!'

The prince, who'd been watching intently, began to struggle against his bonds. He shouted through the gag in his native tongue.

'I'll be decorated with medals and honours,' Otto went on, 'and you two, along with your friend Selene, will be handed over as specimens for live dissection at the Meigwor Exobiological College! How does that sound?!'

'Pretty bad,' Peri admitted.

'Not so cocky now, are you?' Otto smiled again. He extended his long double-jointed arm, to the hitchhiker. 'Kahatama, the weapon!'

The Fooswaylian produced a mega laser-pulse as big as himself. *Where could he have hidden that?* Peri wondered.

Kahatama started to laugh, which was a strange combination of panting and wheezing. He flashed his maroon teeth and pointed the weapon at Peri and Diesel.

'Don't move!' Otto shouted. He took out a laser penknife and zipped through Peri's and Diesel's bonds. They broke apart. Strands of the purple goo were still stuck to them.

'Peri, you will plot a direct course for Meigwor High Command. Diesel, you will be blown to shreds if he doesn't do as he is told.'

The Fooswaylian swivelled and pointed the laserpulse directly at Diesel's head.

'And programme the ship to go into Superluminal mode,' Otto said, 'as soon as the power cells are recharged!'

Peri swallowed. He really didn't like taking orders from Otto. Reluctantly, he went to the control panel and re-engaged the course, shifting from the coordinates for Selene to the ones for the Meigwor High Command. Otto craned his long, thick, crimson neck over Peri's shoulder to watch.

'And now,' Otto said, 'expand a holding cell, if you'd be so good!'

Peri scanned the control panel for the right button, dial or touchpad.

'Get on with it!' Otto shouted.

Then Peri remembered how easy the *Phoenix* made it. 'Holding cell,' Peri said in a voice barely above a whisper.

'Speak up!' Otto demanded. 'I don't think the ship heard you.'

'Holding cell,' Peri said and a portal opened to his left.

'That's it!' Otto bellowed. 'Now, all of you quick march – left right, left right, left right!'

With the Fooswaylian aiming the mega laserpulse at them from the rear, they marched through a white corridor, the

prince shuffling awkwardly because of his
bonds, while Peri and Diesel did their best
not to trip each other up. They reached a
section of wall with a golden image of
a prison gate on it. Otto touched this and
a section of wall slid back.

A bare, smooth-walled oval chamber like
the inside of an egg was revealed.

'In you go!' Otto said and gave his pris-
oners a shove.

As they staggered in, the wall slid shut again.

'Now what?' Diesel asked.

Peri sank to the floor. He put his head in his hands. He felt as if all the hope had drained out of him. He, Selene and Diesel might well be the last survivors of the Milky Way galaxy, if Xion's earlier attack had succeeded. But they weren't going to survive for much longer.

Chapter 7

'What the *prrrip'chiq* are we going to do?' Diesel asked.

Peri roused himself. 'Well, we could untie the prince,' he said.

'Don't waste your time on that Xion lamizoid!' Diesel said. 'We're at war with them, too. Don't you remember how their battleship destroyed the IF Space Station?'

'That's not *his* fault,' said Peri. He turned to Prince Onix. 'We kidnapped you by accident.' Peri explained the mix-up to the prince properly before he ungagged him.

'Thank you,' the prince said. 'I am sorry about the war.'

'Sorry's not good enough,' said Diesel. 'Why did you attack us?'

'My planet was desperate,' the prince said, backing away from the puffed-up half-Martian. 'We are running short of our most important fuel – carbon dioxide. For centuries our enemies the Meigwors

have been stealing this precious resource from us. They use it to heat up their atmosphere – they can't stand even the slightest cold, as you know.'

'Skip the exobiology lesson,' Diesel snapped. 'Why did you attack our galaxy?'

'Because our own CO_2 resources were so depleted we had to look elsewhere. Earth pumps large volumes of CO_2 into its atmosphere, so we began to drill holes and secretly siphon off some of it.'

Peri started to untie the prince. 'That explains the holes in our ozone. It's puzzled Earth scientists for centuries. We used to have global warming, then global cooling . . .'

The prince nodded. 'It would have such an effect, yes. Anyway, our situation did not get better. Siphoning off small quantities from Earth was no longer enough.

Our politicians said we had no choice but to attack and take it all.'

'Seems to me there must have been lots of other choices,' Peri said. 'Why didn't you talk to Earth and the other Milky Way planets – try to make a trade? We are a fair people, you know.'

Prince Onix hung his head. 'I know it was wrong. But there was no time. We thought we were threatened with extinction. Intergalactic negotiations and treaties take years.'

'Yeah, OK, whatever. Enough of that,' Diesel interrupted. 'We have to get out of here.' He pointed at Peri. 'Come on, bionic guts – use that special connection of yours to help us escape.'

Peri shook his head. 'I've lost the connection.'

'What?' Diesel shouted.

'Ever since I was zapped by that electric mace,' Peri explained, 'it's as if my circuits are jumbled.'

Diesel squinted. The strip of hair on his head spiked straight up in the air. 'Maybe you need a reboot, robot.'

Peri frowned. 'What do you mean?'

Diesel didn't answer. Instead, he curled his hand into a fist and punched Peri in the jaw.

Peri saw stars and then his world went black. The next thing he knew, Diesel and Prince Onix were helping him to his feet.

Peri shook his head. He rubbed his sore jaw. 'Why did you do that?'

'Manual reboot,' Diesel said with a smile. 'Did it work?'

Peri did feel as if something had clicked back into place. He wiggled his jaw to make sure nothing was broken. 'You didn't have to hit me so hard.'

Diesel smirked. 'If it worked, that's all that matters.'

Peri took a deep breath and walked to the section of wall that had slid back to admit them. It was completely smooth, no sign of a join. He placed his palms on the wall. It was warm to the touch. A humming noise began in his head. Yes, he could feel something beneath his fingertips, a network of energy lines, running through the wall like arteries and veins. There was a place where the energy lines converged – a hot spot. He pressed. A panel slid silently open. Beneath, he saw a pattern of pulsing lines, red, yellow, blue and green, like spaghetti made of light. He knew, somehow, he had to place his thumb just *there*, breaking the connection between the red light and the blue.

He felt a mild tingling in his thumb as he touched the spot. There was a soft hum. The cell door slid open.

'Well done,' Prince Onix whispered, looking up and down the corridor.

'Took your time about it,' said Diesel.

'We have to beam down to Meigwor to rescue Selene,' Peri said. He felt his energy surge. An idea was forming. He was getting back to his old bionic self. He touched another section of wall. 'Bits and bobs,' he said to the *Phoenix*. 'Unlock.'

The bits and bobs drawer slid out. From a jumble of string, gaffer tape and laser screwdrivers, he pulled out the Xion teleportation band. 'Lucky we've got this!' Peri turned to the prince. 'But you'd better not come. Meigwor isn't safe for you.'

'It isn't safe for us either,' Diesel added.

'If I stay on the ship, the Meigwor and the Fooswaylian will find me,' said Prince Onix, nervously chewing his lip.

'No, they won't,' said Peri. 'Follow me!'

He set off at a run along the corridor. The others followed.

They came to a green-glowing, oval panel set into the wall. 'Com-pad,' Peri explained. 'It's where I talk to the ship.'

He moved his hands over the panel, pushing buttons and flipping switches. The green glow intensified. From somewhere deep in the ship, Peri heard crackling and popping. Then a noise like the twanging of a super-loud and out-of-tune guitar. The ceiling rushed away from them, rising higher and higher until it was far above them like a mauve-tinted sky.

'*Phawwada!*' said Diesel. '*Ambahl'eevabaw!*'

'What is happening?' the prince asked.

'I'm expanding the ship,' Peri explained. 'Max dimensions — it grows to the size of a small planet. Otto will never find you now.'

Prince Onix smiled. 'Impressive.'

'It will also slow the ship so that it won't reach Meigwor any time soon.' Peri strapped the teleportation device to his wrist.

Prince Onix fiddled with a few tiny, nearly invisible dials where the orange button met the band. 'You have to be touching,' Prince Onix explained. 'Then you can go together.'

Diesel took a step away. 'It works on humans and Martians, doesn't it?' he asked.

'I cannot say for certain,' Prince Onix said.

'Come on, Diesel — there's only one way to find out,' Peri said and pressed the button to make his helmet pop up again. Diesel did the same. Peri tapped a few more buttons on the com-pad and typed in a pass code he didn't even know he knew. 'Lowering shields.'

'We want to go here,' Peri showed Prince Onix the long string of letters and numbers that were the coordinates for Selene's last location.

The prince fiddled with the teleportation device again. Peri couldn't see exactly what he was doing. 'I've done the best I can,' the prince said. 'I've also reprogrammed the *Phoenix* as the home base for the device.'

Peri took hold of Diesel's arm.

'Ready?'

'I don't know about this —'

Peri pressed the teleportation button.

Chapter 8

Peri felt a tingling in his guts, like he'd once felt when jumping off the twenty-metre board into the Maelstrom Gelpool at the IFA gymnasium. He seemed to be in a black sky full of stars. Then he realised he *was* the stars. He'd exploded into tiny fragments, but all the tiny fragments were him, somehow.

Then the stars rushed back together — *Whoooomph!* He was in one piece again. He couldn't see or hear anything, but knew that he was falling, falling, falling from a great height . . .

No he wasn't.

He was standing on firm ground. Somewhere very, very hot.

He opened his eyes.

He and Diesel were in the middle of a jungle. Steam rose from the trunks of the tangled, twisted trees with their purple-and-green leaves. Sweat poured down Peri's face.

'*Af-kyot,*' Diesel said. 'It's boiling.'

On the Plexiglas visor of the Expedition Wear helmet was a tiny, blinking red dot. It indicated Selene's whereabouts – she was directly ahead. They began to march towards the dot. Peri felt relief as cool air coursed around his Expedition Wear. The automatic aircon had kicked in.

The going was still difficult. The ground was soft and squelchy. Evil thorns spiked from the branches of the trees. If one of those ripped their suits, they'd be in trouble – the poisonous atmosphere would choke them, even before the heat cooked them.

The cries and shrieks and whistles of Meigwor wildlife rang through the forest. Peri hoped they wouldn't meet anything a) big, b) carnivorous, and c) hungry.

There was a crash in the trees ahead and a nightmarish creature sprang into view. It was bright red, about the size of a chimpanzee, but without the fur. It had hard, shiny skin with huge muscles underneath. It had six arms, which it was using to swing from tree to tree. The most noticeable thing about it was the absence of a head. It had a long neck which ended in a gaping mouth filled with sharp, curved teeth. It sensed Diesel and Otto somehow and came swinging in their direction, grunting.

Peri's SpeakEasy tuned in and the grunts turned into words. 'YUM! DINNER! LOVELY DINNER! TWO DINNERS!'

'*Run!*' shouted Diesel.

The Meigwor mud sucked at their feet. Trees and thorny bushes loomed up before them. The hideous creature's excited grunts were getting louder. There was no way they could outrun it – it was built for the jungle, they weren't.

Suddenly, Peri knew what to do. He reached down for the sparkling button at his ankle and touched it and rose straight up into the air, through the trees. He looked down and saw the creature right behind Diesel.

'ONLY ONE DINNER NOW! BUT STILL YUM!' Peri heard the creature grunt.

'Diesel!' Peri shouted. 'Press the Zero-G button! On your ankle!'

Diesel fumbled for the button. The

creature reached out three of its six arms to grab him.

Diesel touched the button. The creature's paws grasped empty air as the half-Martian sailed up through the trees to join Peri.

Peri heard the creature grunt in disappointment, 'NO DINNER!'

'Good job I found that button in time!' Diesel said.

'Yes,' said Peri, wondering if Diesel might thank him for thinking of it. He wasn't surprised when Diesel didn't.

Walking in Zero-G mode was not easy. They were just above the tree canopy, and their feet had nothing to touch except air. They had to make swimming motions with their arms. Peri remembered learning in science class at the IF Academy that air was a fluid. But it was a very thin fluid. They had to make huge arm-sweeps and take huge strides to get anywhere. But they gradually got the hang of it. Soon the tree canopy was scooting by beneath them.

The blinking dot on Peri's visor got bigger. And bigger. It took shape.

Peri looked down into a clearing below and saw that the dot had become Selene herself.

'There she is!' Diesel said, seeing her too.

Peri touched the Zero-G button again. He began an angled descent into the clearing. The ground came up to meet him and he landed at a run, keeping his balance. Diesel landed beside him, more heavily.

'Selene!' Peri shouted.

Selene turned and stared at them. She didn't say anything. The sunlight shone off her visor, so that Peri couldn't see her face.

'It's us, you dumboid!' Diesel yelled. 'We've come to rescue you.'

Selene raised a small, hand-held laser and fired it at Diesel.

Peri reacted the quickest, diving at Diesel's legs to tackle him clear. The laser beam passed overhead and hit the tree behind them. It burst into flames.

'What's the matter with her? Has she gone crazy?' Diesel asked.

As they scrambled to their feet, Selene aimed the laser again.

Peri rolled to the ground. Another laser beam zipped past.

'Looks like it,' he said.

Zigzagging wildly – as recommended in the chapter on evading enemy fire in *The IFA Field Survival Guide* – they made it into the cover of the trees. The leaves around them flared up in flames. Selene was still firing.

'The heat must have turned her brain,'

Diesel said, still running. 'Let's go back to the ship and leave her behind.'

'No,' Peri said. 'If we can just disarm her, we can reason with her —'

'How are we going to disarm her?' demanded Diesel.

Peri felt in his pocket. 'With this,' he said. In the palm of his hand was the one Paralyside pellet left over from the fight with the Xion guards. 'Activate your Atmos-Filter.'

With his nostril plugs in place, he broke cover. Selene instantly turned the laser on him. He dived to the ground, hurling the pellet at her feet. It detonated with a crack. Grey smoke arose. Selene reeled and fell over.

Peri ran to where she lay and grabbed the handlaser from her. Diesel ran up to join him.

'Selene,' Peri said. 'It's us, Diesel and Peri. Don't you remember? We've come to take you back!'

Selene groggily got to her feet. 'Who is Selene?' the voice beyond the visor said. It was gruff and guttural. It didn't sound anything like their friend.

Which was not surprising. For the first time, Peri got a proper look through the visor of Selene's Expedition Wear helmet. The face that stared back was crimson, blotchy, with a long snakelike neck coiled neatly around its head.

'It's a Meigwor!'

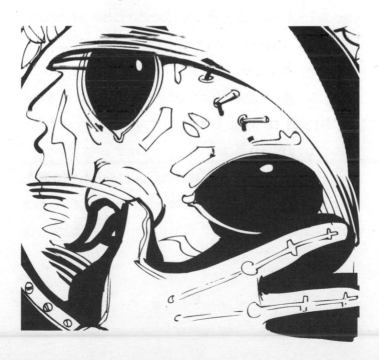

Chapter 9

'What have you done with Selene?' Peri demanded.

'I have done nothing with Selene,' said the Meigwor, his translated voice scratchy through the SpeakEasy. 'I do not know what Selene is.'

Diesel stepped in front of Peri and poked his finger in the Meigwor's chest. 'Where did you get that suit?'

'In trade with a human. For some space-ship parts – a transformational booster a zonkschrift drive and some universal fixative.'

Peri brushed Diesel aside. 'What did this person look like?'

The Meigwor splayed his elbows out like a chicken's. Peri and Diesel looked at each other in surprise. *That must be how a Meigwor shrugs,* thought Peri.

'Of small stature,' the Meigwor started. 'Female gender. Head-growth of considerable length.'

'Sounds like Selene,' Peri said to Diesel. 'But why would she get rid of her suit? And what does she want spaceship parts for?'

Diesel scratched the back of his head. 'Maybe the heat's driven her crazy, like I said.'

'When did you last see her? Was it near here?' Peri asked the Meigwor.

'Not far – she's in that garage over there, see?' The Meigwor pointed to the far side of the clearing where a low, white building was half hidden by overhanging purple-and-green leaves.

'Great!' Peri said. He turned to go, and stopped. 'Can I ask a question?'

'You just did,' said the Meigwor.

'I want to ask another one. Why did you shoot at us?'

'Just Meigwor habit. "See a stranger, shoot a stranger," that's what we say.'

'Right,' Peri said. 'I see. Well . . . You won't mind if I hold on to this handlaser, then? Just to be on the safe side.'

Peri and Diesel ran across the clearing. As they neared the garage, they heard booming voices. Then laughter. Then the noise of some sort of electric drill and the scream of metal on metal.

'I don't like the sound of that,' Peri

said. 'There're Meigwors in there with her. They could be torturing her for fun.'

He set the handlaser to 'fairly painful stun' and kicked open the door.

Selene stood there, flanked by two tall Meigwors. Their snaky, red necks craned curiously towards Peri and Diesel.

Peri hit them with a blast each from the handlaser. The Meigwors crumpled to the floor.

'What did you do that for, space-dunce?' Selene demanded. She was wearing dark blue overalls and had a streak of oil across her cheek. Spaceship parts and tools were scattered all around. At the back of the garage was an old grey flying saucer, scratched and dented.

'We are rescuing you,' Peri said.

Selene snorted. 'Yeah, right.' She knelt

beside the two dazed Meigwors. 'You OK, guys?'

'That really hurt!' said one of them.

'Like stubbing your toe really hard, but all over your body!' said the other.

Selene helped them to their feet.

'She's gone mad,' Diesel muttered to Peri. 'Totally flipped. We have to get her out of here.'

He grabbed Selene and pulled her towards him.

'Back off, you guys!' he warned the Meigwors. 'Or my friend will zap you again.'

'Get off!' said Selene, struggling against Diesel's firm grip.

'Don't worry,' said Diesel soothingly. 'You must have been hypnotised or drugged – but we'll cure you . . .'

Selene elbowed him in the stomach and broke free.

'You total blankoid, Diesel!' she screamed.

'*Grark!* Don't talk to me like that!' Diesel shouted. 'Have you forgotten who I am?'

Peri held up both his hands. 'OK, easy. Both of you.' He turned to Selene and asked, 'What's going on, exactly?'

'Blotto and Blatto are my friends,' Selene said, gesturing to the two Meigwors. They helped me escape from General Rouwgim. They're his enemies, just like we are.'

'But I saw you on the Quikmap monitor,' Peri said. 'You were being attacked — by Meigwors. They had swords and laser-pulses —'

'That was a training exercise,' Selene explained. 'I was running through a few combat scenarios with these guys and their friends.'

'We are working to overthrow the evil Emperor Niatto the Nasty,' said Blotto.

'And Selene's help was invaluable — she certainly knows plenty of tricks!'

Selene nodded. 'That's why they let me have this old flying saucer. I'm trying to fix it up and blast out of here. Except, I can't get it to work.'

'Forget that!' said Diesel. 'We don't have time to mess with that old junk. We've left Otto on the ship, he could be up to anything.'

He threw his arm round Selene's shoulder and grabbed Peri by the arm. He reached for the orange button on the Xion teleportation band.

'Will it work with three —' Peri started but Diesel slammed the button before he could finish his sentence.

'*Woooaaaagh!*' Peri screamed. He felt as if he was being stretched, squashed and shuffled all at once. The air crackled and sparkled and flashed. Something was wrong – there was an enormous field of energy playing around them – but they weren't going anywhere.

All three of them collapsed in a heap. They had not moved. They were still in the garage. The air stopped crackling and sparkling and flashing. Peri began to feel normal.

Almost normal. Had he short-circuited again? He got to his feet and noticed at once that the ground seemed further away than usual. Diesel, who was usually taller than him, was now small enough so that Peri could see the top of his head of long brown hair. But Diesel didn't have long, brown hair. He looked to his right and saw Selene running a hand over her head, which was completely bald – except for the strip of hair running along the middle.

Peri closed his eyes and shook his head. He couldn't be seeing what he was seeing. But he opened his eyes again to the strange jumbled sight. He, Diesel and Selene's bodies had been mixed and matched.

'Uh-oh,' Selene breathed.

Diesel held out a lock of hair that was attached to his head and gazed at it in horror. 'I'm a girl! No!'

'I guess that's what happens when you use technology you don't understand,' said Peri. 'Maybe there's a way to set it for three users, but we didn't –'

'You've got my legs!' Diesel interrupted him. 'Give them back! Right now!'

'How?'

'I'm a short-legged girl!' wailed Diesel.

Peri cautiously checked the rest of himself. It all seemed to be in order . . . *No, wait,* he thought. *My stomach!* It was no longer the firm stomach he was used to. He could push his finger right in. There were no bionic parts under there any more.

Selene saw him touch his stomach and copied the gesture. Her mouth dropped open in shock. 'It feels like there's *metal* under my skin!'

'We got shuffled!' said Peri. 'We have to get off this planet – and hope there's something on the *Phoenix* that'll change us back.'

'There'd better be!' said Diesel. 'I don't want to spend the rest of my life as a girl! With dwarf legs!'

'My legs are normal!' said Peri, annoyed. 'It's yours that are too long.'

Selene picked up a piece of space junk – it looked like an old-fashioned power cell – and carried it over to the flying saucer. 'I'd better have another try at this,' she said.

She banged and clanged about, fitting it under the saucer's bonnet.

'So – you're the Resistance, are you?' said Peri to Blotto, trying to make conversation.

'Yes,' said Blotto. 'Not all Meigwors are cruel and aggressive like Niatto and his mates.'

'Yeah, some of us think that all the intelligent life forms should live together in peace and harmony.'

'But Niatto doesn't like peace,' said Blotto. 'So we don't like him.'

'Hey, guys!' said Selene. 'I think I've cracked it!'

'What?' said Peri. 'That was quick!'

'I know, it's amazing — I suddenly felt I could totally *understand* this machine, I knew exactly what to do and my fingers worked so fast it's as if I was —'

'Bionic,' Peri finished her sentence.

'Yeah,' Selene said.

'Long story,' Peri said. 'I'll tell you later.' Peri found that he missed being bionic.

'Let's go!' Selene said and opened the door of the flying saucer. It was small and cramped inside, and smelt of stinky leather and alien sweat. The controls at the front were sticky with brown and yellow stains. Peri tried not to think about what kind of aliens had been in here before them.

'Goodbye, you guys,' Peri called to the Meigwors. 'Sorry for zapping you!'

'Good luck!' called Selene as she climbed into the flying saucer. It had been designed for only two occupants. When Diesel and Peri piled in after her, they were almost sitting on each other's laps.

'Your hair's in my face!' said Selene.

'It's not my hair, it's *your* hair!' said Diesel.

'Couldn't you have got something bigger?' asked Peri.

'I was lucky to get this,' said Selene. She closed the lid. A single neon strip light flickered on. Selene's fingers raced across the console, touching buttons, as if she was playing the piano, or a Gromboolian Synthesiser.

They began to move. First, the saucer juddered forward, then hovered a few centimetres off the ground. It seemed to drag its way out of the garage, into the clearing, each side dipping and shaking with the motion.

Selene pressed more buttons. 'OK,' she said. 'Here we go.'

She reached for a lever and gently pulled it down. The saucer spun, slowly at first, and then faster and faster. Peri felt a curious tingling in his belly, and realised that he was feeling dizzy and sick. The old-fashioned spaceship didn't have the modern stabilisers that the *Phoenix* had.

Through the tiny porthole, Peri saw Blotto and Blatto down below, waving goodbye. Then the two Meigwors became a blur as the saucer spun and spun, faster and faster. The whole jungle became a blur, looking like someone had spilt water on a painting, making the colours run.

Whooosh! In a couple of nanoseconds they had left the jungle far behind and were hurtling up through the clouds.

'This old wreck can certainly shift!' said Selene.

The sky all around them turned red. An ear-splitting siren wailed. A moment later, the sky was filled with the feared Meigwor Ultracombat craft converging on them. They were black craft with pointed noses. And they were fast.

'We've got company,' Selene said, turning a dial and making the flying saucer drop low, beneath their attackers.

Twin lasers zipped overhead, right where their tiny craft had been a nanosecond before.

'Let's get out of here!' Diesel bellowed.

Inside, Peri tingled with fear. This could be the end. The Meigwors were not out to capture them now; they were out to blow them to pieces. He noticed that Selene's strip of hair had turned a dull grey.

'I'll steer,' said Selene. 'Peri, you take charge of the boosters.'

'What about me?' demanded Diesel.

'You can be lookout.'

'OK – there's one coming straight for us on the starboard side!'

'Thanks,' said Selene, deftly switching course, while Peri pulled both booster levers. The Ultracombat craft passed beneath them and its laser beams streamed away into space.

'Two more above us, to port!' shouted Diesel.

Again, Selene and Peri dodged out of the danger zone. The Ultracombat craft were much more powerful than the tiny flying saucer. But they weren't as mobile.

'One on each side!' screamed Diesel. 'Port and starboard!'

Peri reached over Selene's shoulders to wrench the booster levers up. The flying saucer spun in tight circles, rocketing up higher out of Meigwor's atmosphere.

The two Ultracombat craft fired at the same instant. Their laser beams passed below the flying saucer and hit each other. They both exploded in orange fireballs, propelling the flying saucer even further into outer space.

'Yay!' said Diesel. Peri and Selene briefly took their hands from the controls to high-five each other.

'Look!' said Diesel. 'They're turning back!'

He was right. The Meigwor Ultracombat

craft were wheeling around and diving back to the planet's surface.

Diesel punched the air then flipped Selene's long hair out of his face. 'We did it!'

Selene frowned. 'It's not like the Meigwors to give up so easily. They must have some other trick up their sleeve.'

'Like what?' said Diesel.

Peri's eye fell on the radar screen.

'Like that,' he said.

Two giant rocks, the size of small moons, were heading straight for them.

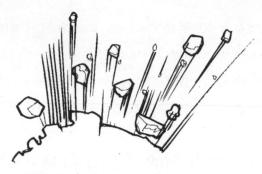

Chapter 10

'Quick!' Diesel shouted. 'Dodge them!'

Peri grabbed the booster levers and tried to calculate a path away from the moon-sized asteroids. Diesel shouted commands and Selene obeyed – slicing left then right. Up and down.

'It's not working,' Selene said, twisting to look at the asteroids advancing on both sides of her. The huge rocks were closing in. 'Look at the size of those things? Here!' She squeezed out of the way. 'You take the controls, Diesel. Peri, do you still have that teleporter?'

Peri gave it to her, keeping one hand on the boosters, pushing the flying saucer higher and faster. 'But . . . it might scramble us up completely this time!'

Selene examined the teleporter closely. She wedged her fingernail at the hinge and cracked it open. 'It was configured for two,' she said, tugging at tiny wires and stripping them with her teeth. Peri was unnerved

as he watched her twist and pinch wires using *his* hands.

His bionic hands.

Peri glanced out of the porthole. One of the rocks was rolling and tumbling in space as it rushed towards them. He glanced out of the other porthole and saw the exact same thing.

'That's it!' said Selene. 'I think.' She clapped one hand on each of her comrades.

I hope this works, thought Peri.

Selene hit the button.

Peri felt the tingling, then the blackness. Then the sensation of fragmenting into millions of tiny stars. Then the rush of energy as all those stars crashed together, and then the falling sensation . . . Then firm ground beneath his feet.

He opened his eyes. He was back on the Bridge of the *Phoenix,* with Diesel and

Selene. Selene had her long brown hair back; Diesel had his strip of hair, and his own legs. Peri touched his stomach. It was firm once more.

'We're back to normal!' he said.

'Look!' Diesel said, pointing to the 360-monitor and the tiny flying saucer they'd just left, an insignificant dot in the vastness of space. The two great asteroids were speeding towards it on a collision course. The flying saucer exploded into billions of fragments that rained in space when the asteroids crashed into one another.

'*F'narg!*' said Diesel. 'That was nearly us!'

'They'll think they got us!' Peri said. 'They won't know that we teleported — they'll stop coming after us now!'

A booming Meigwor voice came over the ship's speakers. 'Earth criminals! This is General Rouwgim! Our sensors have picked up your escape! Return to Meigwor immediately! Bring the prince with you! This is an order! Failure to comply will result in annihilation!'

They stared at each other in alarm. Selene looked at the control panel. 'The Expansion Packs are engaged! You'd better shrink the ship – we make a pretty big target like this!'

Peri waved his hand and the control panel glided into his grasp. His fingers effortlessly flicked across the switches and dials as he downsized the ship.

Immediately, Prince Onix, Otto and Kahatama came tumbling into the Bridge from wherever they had been.

'What happened?' Prince Onix asked, gazing round in confusion.

The little Fooswaylian was holding an enormous laserpulse. He looked like a plum carrying a banana. Otto had a duster.

'Right!' Otto boomed. 'Enough messing about! Turn this ship round and head straight for Meigwor right now – or I'll pulverise you!'

'And then I'll blast you to smithereens!' said the Fooswaylian.

'Return to Meigwor!' boomed General Rouwgim. 'Or be annihilated!'

'OK,' said Peri mildly. 'Fair enough.'

'I'll give you a hand,' said Selene, catching his eye.

'No!' Prince Onix screamed. 'You can't let them take me to Meigwor!'

'Just what do you guys think you're doing?' demanded Diesel.

'They're being sensible!' boomed Otto. 'Giving up the fight in the face of over-whelming force.'

Kahatama sniggered.

'Let me see . . .' Peri muttered, scanning the console.

'Hmm . . .' said Selene.

They looked at each other and nodded.

Peri touched the Eject Hazardous Space Waste button.

At exactly the same time, Selene stroked the Contain Exo-Zoological Specimens touchpad.

Two metal arms shot out of the floor, grabbed Kahatama and turned him upside down. He squeaked and dropped his laserpulse. A trapdoor opened in the floor, leading to a waste disposal chute. The metal arms neatly dropped the Fooswaylian down the chute.

'WAAAAHHHH –' he began; but the rest was cut off by the trapdoor closing.

'What the –' began Otto. A transparent cylinder shot down from the ceiling and imprisoned him, muffling his voice. He beat furiously on the surface.

'Can he break out of that?' Diesel asked.

'No way!' said Peri. 'It's made of super-toughened Venusian silicate – it would hold a wild Aldebaranian Horned Fizzwoggler, or . . .' he glanced at Otto's crimson face and pulsing fists, '. . . or a hysterically angry bounty hunter.'

The voice of the Meigwor general filled the Bridge. 'Despite our warnings you have not changed course for Meigwor! This is an ultimatum: change course or face the consequences!'

'Hey, General!' Selene said. 'I've got a message from Otto!'

'What is the message?' boomed the general.

Selene grinned. 'He says, stick your head under your armpit and take a deep breath!'

'I did not say that!' shouted Otto. But the transparent prison muffled his voice so that the general heard nothing.

'Very well!' came the general's furious, amplified tones. 'Faced with the choice between obedience and painful death, you have chosen painful death. So be it! Otto, the traitor, will suffer the most painful death of all!'

There was a click as the transmission was broken.

'You idiots!' came Otto's muffled roar. 'You don't know what you've done!'

'You might as well team up with us now, Otto,' Peri said. 'Not that you have much choice.'

'We're all dead!' Otto said. 'The general will kill us all!'

'He has to catch us first!' said Selene.

Otto slapped his extra-long arms on the floor of the Bridge. 'He doesn't have to! He'll launch an asteroid at us! And then he'll detonate it by remote control, and it will shatter into a trillion pieces of deadly rock and dust all around us, and we'll get knocked and hit and smashed around – but we'll stay alive, because of the shields. We just won't be able to get anywhere. We'll be trapped in a prison of floating rocks. Then he'll send troops to board us. And then . . .' Otto gulped. 'I can't bear to think about it . . .'

'If you want to avoid that, you'd better help us,' said Peri. 'Put down the duster and we'll let you out.'

Otto placed the duster on the floor. Peri lifted the super-toughened Venusian silicate cylinder off him. Diesel, keeping him covered with the laserpulse, picked up the duster.

'We're going to need to work as a team to do this,' Peri said. 'Diesel, Otto and Prince Onix – you man the guns. We're going to have to blast a path through all this rock and dust and it'll come at us from all sides. I'll take the helm. Selene — stand by to engage Superluminal!'

They all took their positions.

On the monitor, Peri saw another asteroid hurtling towards them — a planet-sized ball of rock, shining silver with the light of Meigwor's distant sun. When it almost filled the monitor screen, it exploded in a blizzard of meteors.

For a moment they all stood spellbound, watching the myriad chunks and shards of rock cartwheel through space.

As the first piece of rock crashed into the *Phoenix*'s shields, Peri staggered, lost his balance and fell to the floor. He saw the others hit the deck too.

Diesel scrambled to the gun turret. He started firing the xenon missiles,

getting the biggest chunks of rock in his sights and blasting them before they could hit the *Phoenix*.

Selene joined Peri at the control panel. He expanded the gun turret. Otto and the prince joined Diesel, and they too began blasting at the deadly rocks.

Selene manipulated the Nav-wheel with breathtaking skill, making the *Phoenix* dive and swoop and swerve to avoid the biggest chunks of rock, which were flying at them from all directions. Some of the smaller ones got through, despite the efforts of Selene and the gun crew. The ship was rocked and jolted and shaken. Peri had to cling on fast to the edge of the control panel to avoid being thrown all over the ship.

How much more of this could the *Phoenix* take?

Peri couldn't engage Superluminal – they needed a clear path through space. Hitting a big rock at Superluminal speed would smash them into a million pieces, and then smash each of those million pieces into a million pieces.

'Concentrate fire at 270 degrees!' shouted Selene. She steered the ship into a channel that was almost clear – just a thin belt of rocks and dust lay before them.

Diesel, Otto and the prince swivelled their cannon in the same direction. They opened fire. Xenon missiles streaked through space ahead of them. A huge rock loomed up in their path. It shattered into fragments as the missiles hit it.

'Now!' Peri shouted.

Selene hit the Superluminal drive.

And everything changed.

The ship stabilised. Peri released his

grip on the console. The rocks disappeared. The only thing left was the blurred streaks of stars as the *Phoenix* shot past.

'Deactivate Superluminal,' Peri said.

'Aye-aye!' Selene said.

They were hanging in the blackness of space, nothing around them for light years. A few distant stars shone with icy beauty.

Peri burst out laughing. Selene and Diesel joined in the laughter. So did Prince Onix. Even Otto was making a strange honking noise.

Peri couldn't believe it. They'd survived another attack, rescued Selene and saved the prince from a fate worse than death. Plus, they'd thwarted the efforts of Xion guards, a treacherous Fooswalyian, a headless jungle predator, evil Meigwors and deadly chunks of asteroid sent to kill them.

'We made it,' said Diesel. 'We're safe!'

'Yup,' said Peri. 'For now . . .'

Can Peri and the crew keep the
Meigwors and the Xions off their trail?

Will they survive when they crash-land
on an unknown planet?

Find out! In . . .

Turn the page to read Chapter 1.

Chapter 1

'We made it!' Diesel cheered. The gunner's narrow band of hair was a happy shade of orange. He wiggled around the Bridge in some strange Martian victory dance.

Even Otto, the Meigwor bounty hunter, looked on the verge of a little smile. His lipless mouth curled upwards like a dying space-slug.

Diesel whooped. 'If I wasn't the most amazing gunner in this galaxy, we'd never have got out of that alive.'

Otto's faint smile faltered. '*I* saved us!'

boomed the Meigwor. 'It was *my* skill that obliterated that massive rock!'

Diesel stopped dancing. His eyes flashed yellow. 'That wasn't skill, it was luck. If it wasn't for me, we'd have been smashed into oblivion.'

Peri couldn't help laughing. With those two arguing, everything was back to normal. Peri high-fived Selene, it was good to have their engineer back and safe. They'd rescued her from the Meigwors, refused to hand over Prince Onix and made a lucky escape from Otto's home planet. The vengeful Meigwor General Rouwgim had created a giant asteroid storm and it had been a team effort to guide the *Phoenix* through it without being pulverised. Diesel and Otto had blasted what they could, while Peri and Selene had navigated the *Phoenix* through the deadly shower of rocks.

'I'll check the damage, while you plan our next move,' Selene said.

Peri smiled. Selene's time in captivity had done nothing for her bossiness. She was even back in her patched spacesuit and had a smudge of grease on her cheek.

'Otto, Diesel, stop arguing,' she snapped. 'I need you to check over the weapons systems to see what needs to be repaired first.' The two gunners glared at her but knew better than to argue. They slouched to the gunnery station.

'Onix,' Selene continued as she pushed past the prince, 'try to stay out of the way.'

'No one talks to the firstborn son and heir to the throne of Xion like that!' the prince said, stiffening, and slicked his webbed fingers through his hair. 'Especially not a girl.'

Peri winced. Onix was in really big trouble. He didn't know Selene. She could use most of the weapons on the *Phoenix*, and she didn't like being treated like a girl. Selene's eyes narrowed like the focusing lens on a DeathRay pulveriser. 'I'm the engineer of this ship and you'll do what you're told or you can find another ride home.'

Onix didn't say a word, but moved as far away from her as he could.

'Right,' Peri said. 'Our priority is to return Prince Onix to Xion.'

'No! We must return to Earth!' Diesel yelled. 'The Emperor will be missing me . . . I mean, us! Earth needs its best Star Fighters back.'

Selene adjusted some nano-dials on the control panel. 'Maybe the prince can tell Xion to stop attacking the Milky Way. Then we can go home.'

Peri clicked his fingers and the control panel slipped from under Selene's hands. It floated towards him. 'First,' he said, 'let's contact Xion and explain that kidnapping Onix was a mistake. We don't need a second planet after us.'

Peri activated the com-pad, flicking a zip-dial to scan all frequencies and automatically connect with planet Xion.

'Hold it!' Otto boomed. 'The Xions will take me prisoner!'

'I'll make sure you get far worse,' mumbled Onix, 'you muscle-bound Meigwor freak.'

Otto pulled a short silver stick from his snakeskin belt and stepped towards the prince. 'What was that, squid-breath? You think these pathetic Earthlings are going to defend *you*?'

'Pathetic?!' Diesel shouted. 'We could beat the entire Meigwor space fleet without breaking a sweat.'

Otto's black tongue shot out and cracked

like a whip in front of Diesel's nose. 'Stay out of it, space-monkey!'

'Never!' Diesel launched himself, grabbing the two lumps on Otto's freakishly long neck as Onix leapt on to the Meigwor's legs. Otto staggered backwards until he lost his balance. Peri sprang from the captain's chair to avoid being hit, but one of Otto's double-jointed elbows slammed into Peri's chest and pinned him against the deck.

'Cosmic squid-brains!' Otto roared. 'Space-monkey slime!'

Peri scrambled free from the fight. Diesel was darting and weaving and trying to punch Otto wherever he could. Otto was trying to shake Onix from his back, but the prince clung on like a space-limpet.

'Meigwor scum,' the prince yelled, as gobs of fishy sweat flew off him. 'Lumpy-necked space-freak!'

Otto was flailing around trying to hit both of them with the silver stick. The weapon was now eleven times longer than it had been. As the Meigwor waved it about, sparks flew everywhere.

Whaacckk! The stick smacked against Peri's arm.

Craackle. A zap of electricity fizzed through him. His muscles and computer circuits twitched uncontrollably, making his eyes

water as his vision shimmered. *The stick is an electro-prod!* he realised.

'Stop it now, before someone gets hurt,' Peri yelled, dodging Otto's electro-prod, Diesel's fists and Onix's sweat. Otto threw Onix from his back, before knocking Diesel and Peri to the deck and pouncing on them. It was going to be hard to break up the fight alone.

'Selene – help!' Peri called.

Peri saw the engineer grab what looked like a ten-centimetre-square piece of pink paper from her tool belt. She dashed towards the prince as he stood up, ready to rejoin the fight. She slapped the paper on his forehead and it stuck. Onix stumbled backwards looking stunned.

'One down, two to go,' Selene muttered, as the prince fell face first on to the deck. 'Sleep well, Your *Highness*.'

'Who's next?' Selene asked and looked from Diesel to Otto. The pair stopped struggling as they glanced at Onix's limp body.

Peri wrestled free from under them and rushed over to the prince. Onix was out cold. 'What have you done?'

Selene snatched the sticky paper from the prince's forehead. 'I call it a Sleepez. Something I invented myself,' she said proudly. 'The adhesive is a sedative. The prince will be out for a few hours.'

'Hours?' Peri said, shaking the prince.

'He got what he deserved,' Selene replied.

'His Royal Majesty, King of Xion,' announced the ship.

Peri looked up. The face of the Xion king dominated the 360-monitor. For a nanosecond, the king looked curious – but then his expression changed to shock and horror. Peri's circuits chilled as he realised what the scene on the Bridge must look like to the king. Peri was kneeling over an unconscious Onix, shaking him.

'What have you done to my son?' the king shouted.

'No,' said Peri, standing up. 'Wait! You don't understand.'

The king looked so angry; Peri felt as if his voice might rattle the *Phoenix*, even from light years away. 'Wicked aliens! You taunt me with my son's dead body! Xion won't stand it! You will pay for this . . . *with your lives!*'